Buggy Bug has
something to say.

. . . is very important.

**Very, very, very,
very, very, very,
very, very, very,
very important.**

Nothing.

Buggy Bug!